I WENT TO THE SUPERMARKET

Paul Howard

For Tiggy

Bloomsbury Publishing, London, New Delhi, New York and Sydney

First published in Great Britain in 2016 by Bloomsbury Publishing Plc
50 Bedford Square, London, WC1B 3DP

A CIP catalogue record for this book is available from the British Library

ISBN 978 1 4088 4468 7 (HB)
ISBN 978 1 4088 4470 0 (PB)
ISBN 978 1 4088 4469 4 (eBook)

Printed in China by Leo Paper Products, Heshan, Guangdong

1 3 5 7 9 10 8 6 4 2

www.bloomsbury.com

All papers used by Bloomsbury Publishing are natural, recyclable products made from wood grown in well-managed forests.
The manufacturing processes conform to the environmental regulations of the country of origin

I went to the **supermarket** and I bought . . .

a pair
of
superhero
pants.

Well...

I went to the **supermarket**

and I bought a pair

of superhero **pants**

and...

a cute baby
ELEPHANT.

I went to the **supermarket** and I bought a pair of superhero **pants**, a cute baby **ELEPHANT** and . . .

a tuba!

Well I went to the supermarket and I bought a pair of superhero pants, a cute baby ELEPHANT, a tuba

and . . .

a fearsome
granny
PIRATE!

I went to the supermarket and I bought a pair of superhero pants,
a cute baby ELEPHANT,
a tuba, a fearsome
granny pirate and some . . .

dancing **A L I**

E N S.

a cute baby ELEPHANT,
a tuba,

a fearsome granny pirate,
some dancing ALIENS
and . . .

a fire-breathing
DRAGON!

I went to the **supermarket** and I bought a pair of superhero **pants**, a cute baby **ELEPHANT**, a **tuba**, a fearsome granny pirate, some dancing **ALIENS**, a fire-breathing **DRAGON** and . . .

whee!
an aeroplane!

Well I went to the
supermarket
and I bought a pair of
superhero pants,
a cute baby ELEPHANT,
a tuba, a fearsome
Granny pirate,
some dancing ALIENS,
a fire-breathing
DRAGON, an
aeroplane
and . . .

a giant pink

FLAMINGO!

I went to the supermarket and I bought a pair of superhero pants, a cute baby ELEPHANT, a tuba, a fearsome granny pirate, some dancing ALIENS, a fire-breathing DRAGON, an aeroplane, a giant pink FLAMINGO and . . .

a mountain of **Jelly!**

Well I went to the

supermarket

and I bought a pair of

superhero **pants**,

a cute baby **ELEPHANT**, a **tuba**,

a fearsome granny pirate,

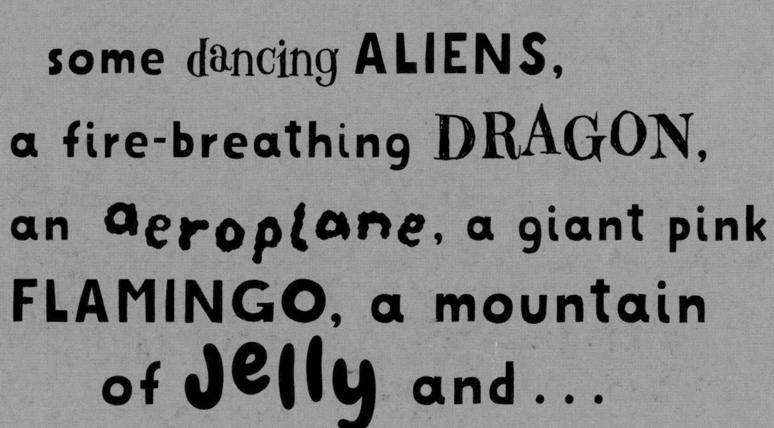

some dancing **ALIENS**,

a fire-breathing **DRAGON**,

an *aeroplane*, a giant pink

FLAMINGO, a mountain

of **jelly** and . . .

POP
bubbles!

I went to the
supermarket
and I bought . . .
a pair of
superhero pants,

a cute baby
ELEPHANT,

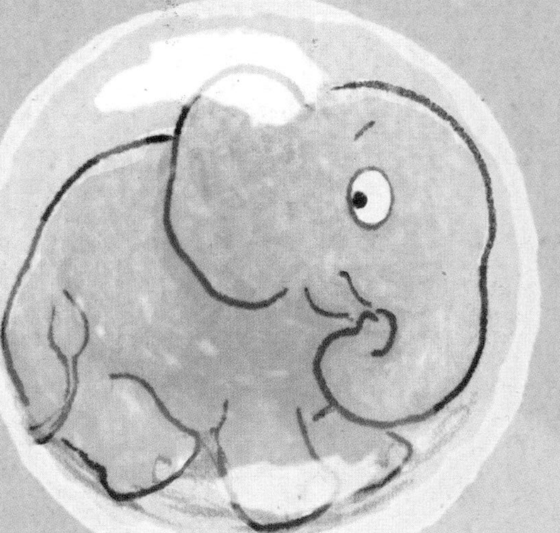

a tuba,

POP

a fearsome
granny
pirate,

pop

some dancing
ALIENS . . .

pop

a fire-breathing
DRAGON,
an aeroplane,
POP

a giant
pink
FLAMINGO
and – er –
bubbles!

POP

Ha! Ha! I win.
You forgot something.

Did I?
What was it?

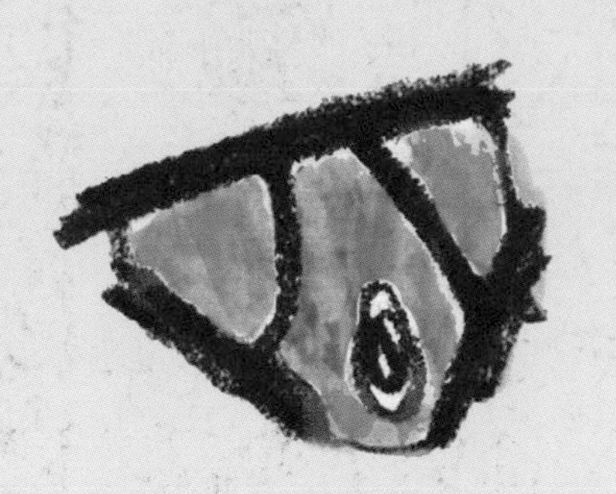

a pair of superhero pants,

a cute baby ELEPHANT,

a tuba,

a fearsome granny pirate,

some dancing
ALIENS,

a fire-breathing
DRAGON,

an aeroplane,

a giant pink
FLAMINGO,

bubbles and . . . and . . . and . . .

splat!
Oh, yes it was
the Jelly!
Silly me . . .
I win!